TACKY
the Penguin

Helen Lester
Illustrated by Lynn Munsinger

M

MACMILLAN CHILDREN'S BOOKS

First published in U.S.A. by Houghton Mifflin

First published in United Kingdom 1991 by Pan Macmillan Children's Books
This Picturemac edition published 1993 by Pan Macmillan Children's Books
a division of Pan Macmillan Publishers Limited
Cavaye Place London SW10 9PG
and Basingstoke

Associated companies throughout the world

ISBN 0–333–58334–5

Text Copyright © 1988 Helen Lester
Illustrations Copyright © 1988 Lynn Munsinger

The right of Helen Lester and Lynn Munsinger to be identified as the
author and illustrator of this work has been asserted by them in accordance
with the Copyright, Designs and Patents Act 1988.

1 3 5 7 9 8 6 4 2

A CIP catalogue record for this book is available from
the British Library

Printed in Hong Kong

There once lived a penguin.
His home was a nice icy land he shared
with his companions.

His companions were named
Goodly, Lovely, Angel, Neatly, and Perfect.

His name was Tacky.
Tacky was an odd bird.

Every day Goodly, Lovely, Angel, Neatly, and Perfect greeted each other quietly and politely.

Tacky greeted them with a hearty slap on the back
and a loud "What's happening?"

Goodly, Lovely, Angel, Neatly, and Perfect always marched

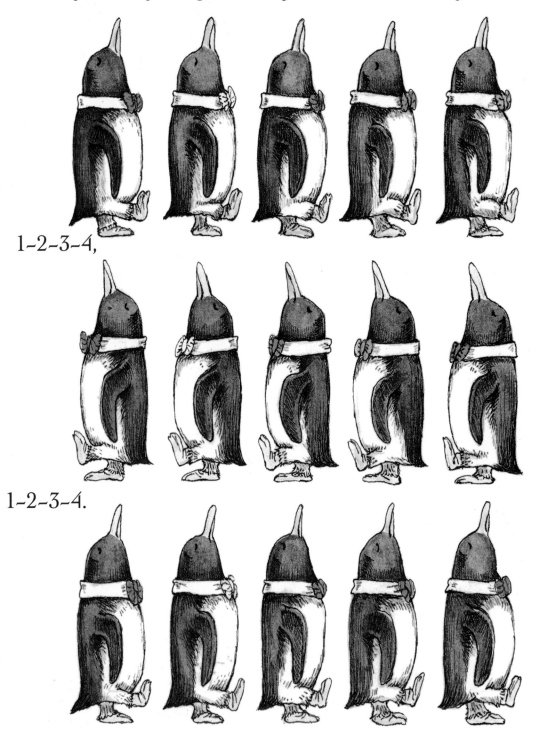

1-2-3-4,

1-2-3-4.

Tacky always marched 1–2–3,

4–2,

3–6–0,

2½,

0.

His companions were graceful divers.

Tacky liked to do splashy cannonballs.

Goodly, Lovely, Angel, Neatly, and Perfect
always sang pretty songs like
"Sunrise on the Iceberg."

Tacky always sang songs like
"How Many Toes Does a Fish Have?"
Tacky was an odd bird.

One day the penguins heard the *thump . . . thump . . . thump*
of feet in the distance.
This could mean only one thing.
Hunters had come.

They were rough and tough, and they came with maps and traps and rocks and locks and long springy switches. As the *thump . . . thump . . . thump* drew closer, the penguins could hear the growly voices chanting,

"We're out to catch some pretty penguins,
And we'll march 'em with a switch,
And we'll sell 'em for a dollar,
And get rich, rich, RICH!"

Goodly, Lovely, Angel, Neatly, and Perfect
ran away in fright.

They hid behind a block of ice.

Tacky stood alone.
The hunters marched right up to him, chanting,
   "We're out to catch some pretty penguins,
   And we'll march 'em with a switch,
   And we'll sell 'em for a dollar,
   And get rich, rich, RICH!"

"What's happening?" blared Tacky, giving one hunter an especially hearty slap on the back.

They growled, "We're hunting for penguins.
That's what's happening."

"PENNNNGUINS?" said Tacky. "Do you mean those
birds that march neatly in a row?"
And he marched,

1-2-3,

4-2,

3-6-0,

2½,

0.

The hunters looked puzzled.

"Do you mean those birds that dive so gracefully?"
Tacky asked.

And he did a splashy cannonball.
The hunters looked wet.

"Do you mean those birds that sing such pretty songs?"
Tacky began to sing, and from behind the block of ice
came the voices of his companions,
all singing as loudly and dreadfully as they could.

"HOW MANY TOES DOES A FISH HAVE?

AND HOW MANY WINGS ON A COW?

I WONDER. YUP,

I WONDER."

The hunters could not stand the horrible singing.
This could not be the land of the pretty penguins.
They ran away with their hands clasped tightly over their ears,
leaving behind their maps and traps and rocks and locks,
and not looking at all rough and tough.

Goodly, Lovely, Angel, Neatly, and Perfect hugged Tacky.
Tacky was an odd bird but a very nice bird to have around.